This book belongs to

....

Walt Disney's

Three Little Pigs

Storybook Favourites

Reader's Digest Young Families

Walt Disney's

Three Little Pigs

Illustrations by The Walt Disney Studios

Story adapted by Milt Banta and Al Dempster

Once upon a time there were three little pigs who went out into the big world to build their homes and seek their fortunes.

The first little pig did not like to work at all. He quickly built himself a house of straw.

Then off he danced down the road, to see how his brothers were getting along.

The second little pig was building himself a house, too. He did not like to work any better than his brother, so he had decided to build a quick and easy house of sticks.

Soon it was finished, too. It was not a very strong little house, but at least the work was done. Now the second little pig was free to do what he liked.

What he liked to do was to play his fiddle and dance. So while the first little pig tooted his flute, the second little pig played his fiddle, dancing as he played.

And as he danced he sang:

'I built my house of sticks,
I built my house of twigs.
With a hey diddle-diddle
I play on my fiddle,
And dance all kinds of jigs.'

Then off danced the two little pigs down the road together to see how their brother was getting along.

The third little pig was a sensible little pig. He was building a house, too, but he was building his of bricks. He did not mind hard work, and he wanted a strong little house, for he knew that in the woods nearby there lived a big bad wolf who liked nothing better than to catch little pigs and eat them up!

So slap, slosh, slap! Away he worked, laying bricks and smoothing mortar between them.

'You can laugh and dance and sing,' their busy brother called after them, 'but I'll be safe and you'll be sorry when the wolf comes to the door!'

‘Ha ha ha! Ho ho ho!’ laughed the two little pigs again, and they disappeared into the woods.

Just as the first pig reached his door, out of the woods popped the big bad wolf!

The little pig squealed with fright and slammed the door.

'Little pig, little pig, let me come in!' cried the wolf.

'Not by the hair of my chinny-chin-chin!' said the little pig.

'Then I'll huff and I'll puff, and I'll blow your house in!' roared the wolf.

And he did. He blew the little straw house all to pieces!

Away raced the little pig to his brother's house of sticks. No sooner was he inside, when there came a Knock, Knock, Knock at the door! It was the big bad wolf!

But of course, the little pigs would not let him come in.

‘Ha ha ha! Ho ho ho!’ laughed the two little pigs. ‘We fooled him.’

Then they danced around the room.

Soon there came another knock at the door. It was the big bad wolf again, but he had covered himself with a sheepskin, and was curled up in a big basket, looking like a little lamb.

'Then I'll huff and I'll puff, and I'll blow your house in!' cried the angry old wolf.

So he huffed
and he PUFFED
and he *puffed*
and he HUFFED,
and he blew the little twig house all to pieces!

Away raced the two little pigs, straight to the third little pig's house of bricks.

'Don't worry,' said the third little pig to his two frightened little brothers. 'You are safe here.' Soon they were all singing gaily.

This made the big bad wolf quite furious!

‘Now by the hair of my chinny-chin-chin!’ he roared,
‘I’ll huff, and I’ll puff, and I’ll blow your
house in!’

So the big bad wolf huffed and he PUFFED,
and he *puffed* and he HUFFED,
but he could not blow down that little house of bricks!
How could he get in? At last he thought of the chimney!

So up he climbed, quietly. Then with a snarl, down
he jumped – right into a pot of boiling water!

With a yelp of pain he sprang straight up the chimney again and raced away into the woods. The three little pigs never saw him again and spent their time in the strong little brick house singing and dancing merrily.

Walt Disney's Three Little Pigs is a *Disney Storybook Favourites* book

Story adapted by Milt Banta and Al Dempster. Illustrations by The Walt Disney Studios.

This edition was adapted and published in 2009 by
The Reader's Digest Association Limited
11 Westferry Circus, Canary Wharf, London E14 4HE

Editor: Rachel Warren Chadd
Designer: Louise Turpin
Design consultant: Simon Webb

We are committed both to the quality of our products
and the service we provide to our customers.
We value your comments, so please do contact us on
08705 113366 or via our website at
www.readersdigest.co.uk
If you have any comments or suggestions
about the content of our books, email us at
gbeditorial@readersdigest.co.uk

Printed in China

A Disney Enterprises/Reader's Digest Young Families Book

ISBN 978 0 276 44467 8
Book code 641-026 UP0000-1
Oracle code 504400016H.00.24